# The Most Wonderful Thing in the World

written by
**Vivian French**

illustrated by
**Angela Barrett**

CANDLEWICK PRESS

$O$*nce, in the time* of your grandmother's grandmother, there was a kingdom. In the middle of the kingdom was a large lagoon dotted with islands, and here a city had been built, a city of sky-blue water and golden bridges. It was a small city, but it was beautiful, and the king and the queen were very proud of it. They were also proud of their daughter, Lucia, and they loved her so much they seldom let her go outside the palace walls.

"How fortunate we are to have such a truly wonderful daughter," said the queen.

"And the day will come," said the king,
 "when Lucia will rule the kingdom."
"Lucia?" The queen rubbed her nose
in a very unqueenly way. "I suppose
she will. But then who will be king?"
The king looked puzzled. "My dear!
Her husband will, of course," he said.
The queen rubbed her nose again.
"But our daughter has no husband."
The king folded his arms and frowned.
"Then we must find her one at once.
We will send a letter to Wise Old Angelo,
who lives on the smallest of the islands.
He will tell us exactly what we should do."

Dear Wise Old Angelo,

We wish to find a suitable husband for our daughter, Lucia.

Please advise us of the best way to go about this difficult task.

Yours in hope,

HRH Bertram and HRH Rachella

P.S. Expense is no object.

Dear Majesties,

I have thought long and hard about what you ask,
and here is my conclusion. You must find the young man
who can show you the most wonderful thing in the world.
He will be the right husband for Princess Lucia.

Yours most sincerely,

*Angelo*

Angelo

Angelo gave his letter to his grandson, Salvatore. Salvatore tucked it in his pocket and rowed across the lake to the royal palace. He knocked on the door, and a servant opened it.

"A message for Their Majesties," Salvatore said.

The king and the queen were delighted.

"The most wonderful thing in the world!" the queen exclaimed. "How very clever!"

The king nodded. "We must send out a proclamation at once. Call the messengers!"

"And is Lucia to know what we are doing, my dear?" asked the queen. "Will she help us choose?"

The king looked thoughtful. "It should be a surprise. We will send her away—"

"Send her away?" The queen was horrified. "Never!"

"She must go," said the king.

"No, no, no!" said the queen.

"Yes, yes, yes!" said the king.

The king and the queen continued to argue.

Neither of them noticed the princess sitting reading in the gallery above them. As their voices grew louder, she closed her book and listened.

The princess came down to the throne room.

"Dearest Ma, dearest Pa," she said, "are you arguing?"

"Certainly not," said the king.

"Arguing?" said the queen. "The very idea!"

"Good." Lucia smiled. "Because I'd like to ask a favor. One day—and I hope it won't be for a long time— I'll be queen. So I would like to explore our city, and—"

The princess never got to finish her sentence. Her father and mother were looking at her as if she had said something amazingly clever.

"Of course, my darling!" said the queen. "Take the royal coach whenever you want."

"Absolutely, my sweet!" said the king. "Use the royal barge as often as you like."

"Thank you," said Lucia. And before her parents could change their minds, she hurried out of the room.

As Lucia came running
out of the palace, she saw
Salvatore sitting on the wall,
playing with a little tabby cat.
"Excuse me," she said, pulling
her cloak closer to cover her
silk dress, "do you know the city?"
Salvatore smiled proudly. "Of course!
I have lived in the kingdom all my life.
Nobody knows the city better than I do,
pretty lady. North, south, east, and west."
"Can you show it to me?" Lucia asked. "Today?"

Salvatore was surprised.
"But it would take longer
than a day. Much longer."
The princess put her hand
on his coat sleeve. "Please?"
The young man bowed low.
"I am Salvatore, pretty lady,
and I am entirely at your service.
Today, tomorrow, and the next day,
until you have seen all that you want."
"Thank you," said the princess, and they
walked away toward the heart of the city.

The first of the suitors came to the palace the next day.

He brought a hundred roses and a blue-tailed lovebird.

"Very beautiful," said the queen.

"But not the most wonderful thing in the world," said the king.

The second suitor brought a snow-white horse.

"Very beautiful," said the king.

"But not the most wonderful thing in the world,"

said the queen.

Day by day, more and more suitors came to the palace.
Each brought something more wonderful than the last.
There were acrobats and airships, pyramids and performing dogs,
mysterious magical beasts and a piece of frozen sky.

The king and the queen were too busy to notice that their daughter
was out all day, every day. When they saw her, she looked happy,
and that was enough. Suitors were arriving every hour,
and there was no time to worry about anything else.

While the king and the queen were busily crossing off suitors from their list, Lucia and Salvatore were wandering the streets of the city. High and low they went, looking at the gilded churches, the glittering arcades of shops, and the sparkling fountains in the wide piazzas paved with stone.

They walked through bustling markets where golden oranges were heaped in piles, and under grand marble arches; they gazed at velvet-curtained mansions and balconies festooned with flowers; and they counted the tall towers of the city cathedral.

Day by day, more, more, and yet more suitors arrived.
The king and the queen grew gray with exhaustion, but still nothing
the suitors brought seemed to be the most wonderful thing in the world.

Not the dancing girls or the airplane,
not the mammoth tusk or the wind machine—
not even the mermaid in a tank.

Once Salvatore had shown the princess the well-known sights,
he took her to the hidden heart of the city, to the places
where the grand never thought to go. Up and down they drifted,
in and out of the sunshine and shadows.
"I never knew there were so many things to see,"
the princess said as Salvatore walked her home to the palace
late one evening. "Where shall we go tomorrow?"
"We've been everywhere," Salvatore told her. "There's nowhere else to go."
"Oh." Lucia stopped smiling. "Are you sure?"

Salvatore looked out over the sky-blue waters of the lake
to his own little island. "Well . . . there could be one more place."
"Then I'll see you tomorrow morning, Salvatore," Lucia said,
and she ran through the tall iron gates.
A messenger was coming out, and he bowed low as she passed.
"Good evening, Your Highness."
Salvatore heard him. "Excuse me!" He caught at the messenger's sleeve.
"Excuse me! What did you say? Who was that girl?"
The messenger stared. "Her Highness Princess Lucia, of course."

As Salvatore rowed home that night, his face was wet with tears.
When he reached the island, he hurried to find Old Angelo.
"Grandfather! What shall I do? I've met a girl, and I love her.
I love her so much, but I can never marry her!"
The old man peered over his spectacles. "Why not?"
Salvatore groaned. "She's a princess. The princess Lucia!"

Old Angelo took off his spectacles, rubbed them clean, and put them back on again. "It seems to me that the answer is easy. You must show the king and queen the most wonderful thing in the world, and then Princess Lucia will be yours."

"But, Grandfather," Salvatore said, "I'm not a prince, or a duke, or an earl." And he walked away, his heart heavy.

The king and the queen also had heavy hearts. The last of the suitors had sailed away to his kingdom, his weapons of mass destruction rejected.

"How can anyone believe weapons are the most wonderful thing in the world?" asked the queen.

The king shrugged. He was too tired to answer.

"So we agree?" said the queen. "No more suitors?"

"No more," said the king. "Absolutely, completely, and utterly no more." And he closed his eyes.

"We should find Lucia," said the queen.

They went to look for the princess, but she was not in her rooms, nor anywhere in the palace.

"Perhaps she's gone out in the coach," suggested the king, but the coach was in the courtyard.

"She must have taken the barge," said the queen, but the barge was by the quay.

The king and the queen began to feel anxious. "Has anyone seen the princess?" they asked. "Where can she be?"

The captain of the barge stepped forward. "I saw her early this morning, Your Majesties. She went out to Old Angelo's island with his grandson."

"Old Angelo? Our daughter has gone to see Old Angelo?" The king looked at the queen. "But why? What is she thinking?"

The queen shook her head. "Who knows? Perhaps we should go and find out, my dear."

"Good plan!" said the king, and the barge was made ready as quickly as possible.

Lucia was walking around the island, Salvatore by her side.
He had met her that morning as arranged but had been
unusually quiet as he rowed her across the water.
Now she asked him if anything was wrong.
He shook his head. "Nothing, Your Highness."
The princess looked at him in surprise. "Your Highness?"
Salvatore sighed, but before he could say anything, there was
a fanfare of trumpets. The king and the queen had arrived.
Old Angelo hurried to receive his royal visitors,
the princess close behind him.
Salvatore followed slowly. He watched the king and the queen
hug their daughter, as if they would never let her go,
and as he watched, he grew thoughtful.

With a low bow, he stepped forward.

"Your Majesties," he said, "I believe I have found—"

The queen sank onto a bench and began to fan herself.

"Oh, how tired I am," she said. "How very, very tired."

Salvatore bowed for the second time.

"Your Majesties, I believe I have found—"

The king sat down beside the queen.

"Exhausted. That's what we are. Exhausted."

Salvatore took a deep breath. "Your Majesties! I have found the most wonderful thing in the world!"

The queen leaned toward the king. "He doesn't look like any of the others, my dear."

"No," the king agreed. "Let's hear what he has to say."

For the third time, Salvatore bowed.

Then he took the princess by the hand. "Here," he said.

"Here is the most wonderful thing in the world."

The queen gave a little gasp and clapped her hands.

"Oh! Oh! Oh, of course she is!"

The king said nothing for a moment, and then he nodded.

"The young man is quite right. Well done. Well done, indeed!"

Lucia took Salvatore's other hand.

"Thank you," she said, and she kissed him.

Lucia and Salvatore were married with all the pomp
and ceremony that is usual when a princess marries.
Your grandmother's grandmother would remember it.
And she would also remember that they ruled their kingdom
wisely and well. They often walked the streets and alleyways
of the city, and they spoke with the people every day.
The people loved them so much that a statue was built
in their honor in the main piazza, and there it still stands.
Lucia and Salvatore are holding their firstborn child,
and underneath, carved in the stone, are the words

*The Most Wonderful Thing*
*in the World.*

For Lia

with love

First U.S. edition 2015

Library of Congress Catalog Card Number 2014953065
ISBN 978-0-7636-7501-1

15 16 17 18 19 20 WKT 10 9 8 7 6 5 4 3 2 1

Printed in Shenzhen, Guangdong, China

This book was typeset in Brioso Pro.
The illustrations were done in watercolor.

Candlewick Press
99 Dover Street
Somerville, Massachusetts 02144

visit us at www.candlewick.com